JAN 0 6 2011

ELK GROVE VILLAGE PUBLIC LIBRARY

3 1250 00929 8906

14/12

14

Y0-ASL-568

Discarded By Elk Grove
Village Public Library

ELK GROVE VILLAGE PUBLIC LIBRARY
1001 WELLINGTON AVE
ELK GROVE VILLAGE, IL 60007
(847) 439-0447

This book belongs to:

_____

Spotty – the quiet dog

Woofy – the noisy dog

Spotty – the quiet dog

Woofy – the noisy dog

Woofy – the noisy dog

Spotty – the quiet dog

Woofy – the noisy dog

Spotty – the quiet dog

To my sister,
Alison, and
our noisy dogs!
S.E.

To Sara —
you're a star!
A.B.

First published in Great Britain in 2009 by Andersen Press Ltd., 20 Vauxhall Bridge Road, London SW1V 2SA.
Published in Australia by Random House Australia Pty., Level 3, 100 Pacific Highway, North Sydney, NSW 2060.
Text copyright © Sue Eves, 2009. Illustration copyright © Ailie Busby, 2009
The rights of Sue Eves and Ailie Busby to be identified as the author and illustrator of this work have been asserted by them
in accordance with the Copyright, Designs and Patents Act, 1988.
All rights reserved. Colour separated in Switzerland by Photolitho AG, Zürich.
Printed and bound in Singapore by Tien Wah Press.

10   9   8   7   6   5   4   3   2   1

British Library Cataloguing in Publication Data available.

ISBN 978 1 84270 829 3 (hardback)
ISBN 978 1 84270 939 9 (paperback)

This book has been printed on acid-free paper

The Quiet Woman and the NOISY DOG

SUE EVES

AILIE BUSBY

ANDERSEN PRESS

In a quiet house, in a **noisy** town,
Lived a quiet woman, and a **noisy** dog.

Woof! Woof!

The quiet woman and her noisy dog
Walked down a quiet street to a quiet park with a pond.

Woof! Woof!

She fed some bread to the **noisy** ducks
And threw a ball for her **noisy** dog,

"Woofy! Fetch!"

Quack!
Quack!

A quiet dog came back with the ball.
The quiet woman patted the quiet dog.

"Good dog!"

The noisy dog came back with a noisy woman,

"Naughty dog, Spotty!
Not your ball!
Not your ball at all!"

Woof!
Woof!

The quiet woman smiled and said, "Let them play!"
The noisy woman said, "O.K!"

The quiet woman and the noisy woman walked. The noisy dog and the quiet dog played (until they were as noisy and as muddy as each other).

Yap! Yap!

Woof! Woof!

The quiet woman and the noisy woman laughed,
"Mucky Pups!"
And called their dogs away.

"Bye!"   "Bye!"

The *quiet woman*
Went into the noisy town
With her muddy dog
And back to her *quiet* house.

The **noisy** woman
Went down the **noisy** street
With *her* muddy dog
And back to her **noisy** house.

Hello!

Hi!

Hey!

Meow!

Tweet! Tweet!

Oink! Oink!

The quiet woman gave her muddy dog a bath.

"Oh! No!"

It was the quiet dog and not her dog at all!

The **noisy** woman gave her muddy dog a bath.

It was the **noisy** dog without any spots at all!

In the quiet house
The quiet woman played with the quiet dog.

"Good dog, Spotty!"

...the quiet dog was noisy in the quiet house,

and the noisy dog was quiet in the noisy house.

Because they wanted to go home.

The quiet woman patted the quiet dog.
She read his tag. "Spotty, Noisy House, Noisy Street,
Noisy Town."

She went out of her quiet house
Into the **noisy** town,

Hey! **Oi!** Vroom! Vroom! Beep! **Beep!**

To take the quiet dog home.

The **noisy** woman hugged her quiet dog.
The quiet woman hugged her **noisy** dog.

"Hello, Spotty!"

"Hello, Woofy!"

The noisy woman and the quiet woman hugged each other,
The quiet woman and her noisy dog
Went out of the noisy house.

"Bye!"

"Thank you! Bye!"

That night,
In the **noisy** town,
In the **noisy** house,
The **noisy** woman slept quietly,
Because she was too tired to be **noisy**.

Ruffle!
Ruffle!

Prrrrrrrrrrr

Sshhhhhhh!

Snuffle!
Snuffle!

Zzzzzzzzzzz!

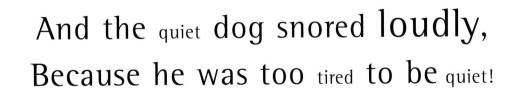

And the quiet dog snored loudly,
Because he was too tired to be quiet!

In the **noisy** town, in the quiet house,
The quiet woman sang **noisily**,

"Oh Woofy! Oh Woofy! I love you, Woofy!
La-La-La-La-La!"

Because she was too
happy to be quiet.

And the **noisy** dog slept _{quietly,}
Because he was so **happy** to be **home!**

Shhhhhhhhhhhhhhhhhhhhhhhhhhhhhhhhhhh!

Woofy – the noisy dog

Spotty – the quiet dog

Woofy – the noisy dog

Spotty – the quiet dog

Woofy – the noisy dog

Spotty – the quiet dog

Spotty – the quiet dog

Woofy – the noisy dog

OTHER BOOKS YOU MIGHT ENJOY:

The Boy Who Lost His Bellybutton

The Gordon Star

Matty in a Mess!

Minty and Tink

When Lulu Went to the Zoo